REPTILE ADVENTURES

Published in 2018 by Windmill Books,
an Imprint of Rosen Publishing
29 East 21st Street, New York, NY 10010

Copyright © 2018 Blake Publishing

Cover and text design: Leanne Nobilio
Editor: Vanessa Barker

Photography: All images © Dreamstime.
Inside back cover illustration by Kim Webber.

Cataloging-in-Publication Data
Names: Johnson, Rebecca.
Title: Gorgeous Geckos / Rebecca Johnson.
Description: New York : Windmill Books, 2018. | Series: Reptile
     adventures | Includes index.
Identifiers: ISBN 9781508193630 (pbk.) | ISBN 9781508193593
     (library bound) | ISBN 9781508193678 (6 pack)
Subjects: LCSH: Geckos--Juvenile literature.
Classification: LCC QL666.L245 J65 2018 | DDC 597.95'2--dc23

Manufactured in China
CPSIA Compliance Information: Batch BW18WM: For Further Information
contact Rosen Publishing, New York, New York at 1-800-237-9932

CONTENTS

I am a gecko.
Have you seen me?

On a wall,
on a window,
or behind your TV?

I am a house gecko,
but it is true,

there are thousands
of types in the wild, too.

On every continent
where it is warm,

you'll find geckos like me,
in many different forms.

Please meet my cousins,
their colors are bright.

Some come out in daylight,
some come out at night.

All types of geckos
have eyes like glass balls.

We lick our eyes clean—most have no lids at all!

We are all geckos, and we hunt for our prey.

We shoot out our tongues
and gulp bugs away.

Cockroaches, mosquitos, and many more pests—

we clean them all up,
without sprays and the rest.

All sorts of geckos
have a magic grip.

Our feet have setae
so that we don't slip.

Because we are reptiles,
we shed our skin

if it starts to get
a bit snug within.

Around the world,
we are kept as pets.

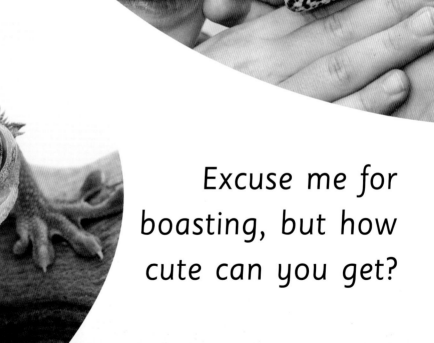

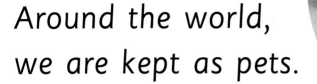

Excuse me for
boasting, but how
cute can you get?

We do a great job,
from the mountains to the sea.
We keep insect numbers down
in the wild, you see.

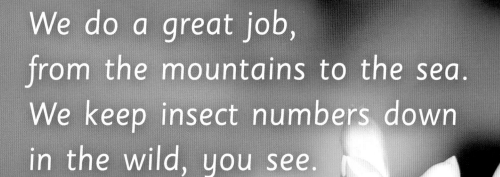

So when you see geckos,
please don't assume

that the only type
is the one in your room!

GLOSSARY

boasting to talk about something with pride

grip to hold onto something very tightly

gulp to eat very quickly by swallowing large pieces of food

hunt to search for something

pests insects that are annoying and cause damage or harm

prey an animal that is hunted for food by another animal

setae stiff, hair-like parts on the bottoms of a gecko's feet

shed to get rid of or to lose from one's body

snug to fit closely

Gecko

FACT ① Stores fat in its tail

FACT ② Has excellent hearing

FACT ③ Is nocturnal

FACT ④ Eats fruit, flower nectar, and insects